To Odie and Rex

I LIKE TO READ is a registered trademark of Holiday House, Inc.

Copyright © 2015 by Michael Garland
All Rights Reserved
HOLIDAY HOUSE is registered in the U.S. Patent and Trademark Office.
Printed and Bound in April 2015 at Tien Wah Press, Johor Bahru, Johor, Malaysia.
The artwork was created with pencil and digital tools.
www.holidayhouse.com
First Edition
1 3 5 7 9 10 8 6 4 2

Library of Congress Cataloging-in-Publication Data
Garland, Michael, 1952- author, illustrator.
Lost dog / Michael Garland. — First edition.
pages cm. — (I like to read)
Summary: A walrus, a whale, penguins, and others help Pete the dog
get to Grandma's house.
ISBN 978-0-8234-3429-9 (hardcover)
[1. Dogs—Fiction. 2. Animals—Fiction. 3. Lost children—Fiction.] I. Title.
PZ7.G18413Lo 2015
[E]—dc23
2014044160

ISBN 978-0-8234-3430-5 (paperback)

LOST DOG

MICHAEL GARLAND

I Like to Read®

Holiday House / New York

To Grandma
Happy Birthday!
Love, Pete

Pete went to see Grandma.
She lived on Mutt Street.

"Too many cars," said Pete.
He got off the road.

EXIT 18

Pete was lost.

"Where is Mutt Street?"
said Pete.
"That way," said the bear.

"That way," said the bird.

"That way," said the big cat.

"That way," said the walrus.

"That way," said the penguins.

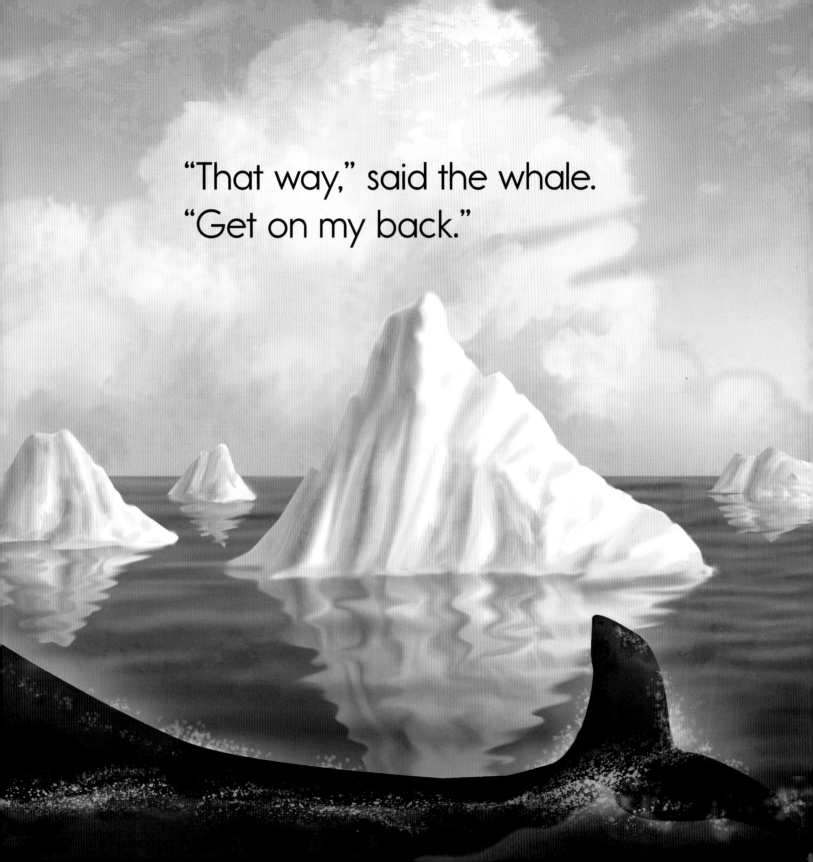

"That way," said the whale.
"Get on my back."

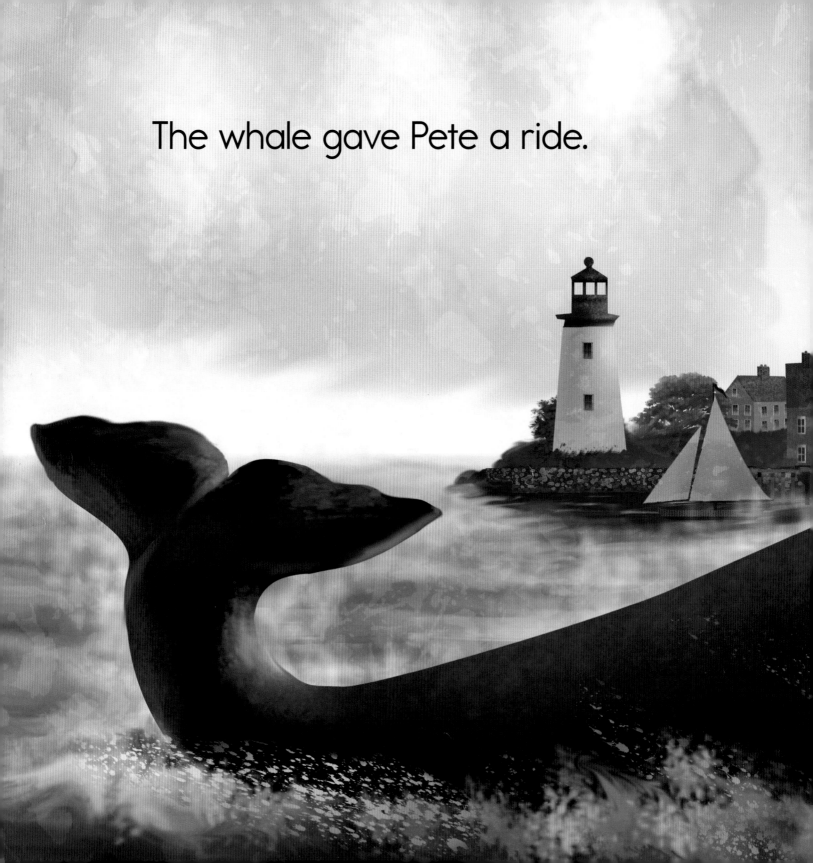

The whale gave Pete a ride.

"Where is Mutt Street?"
Pete said.
"You are on Mutt Street,"
said Officer Bark.

And he was!
"Happy birthday, Grandma!"